THE TRAVELING MEN OF BALLYCOO

EVE BUNTING

THE TRAVELING MEN
OF
BALLYCOO

illustrated by KAETHE ZEMACH

HARCOURT BRACE JOVANOVICH, PUBLISHERS   SAN DIEGO   NEW YORK   LONDON

Printed in the United States of America

LIBRARY OF CONGRESS CATALOGING IN PUBLICATION DATA
Bunting, Eve, 1928-
The traveling men of Ballycoo.
SUMMARY: Although as time goes on, they grow too old to
stay on the road visiting all the small Irish towns, the three
traveling men find a way to bring their music to the people.
[1. Musicians—Fiction] I. Zemach, Kaethe, ill. II. Title.
PZ7.B91527Tr 1983 [Fic] 82-15799
ISBN 0-15-289792-5

First edition

B C D E

Cathal, Sean, and Jimmy O'Malley were the Traveling Men, and there were those who said they were maybe the greatest Traveling Men that Ireland had ever seen.

They had no place that they called home, though Simey
Rooney had left them a cottage in Ballycoo when he passed on.
No matter. The whole length of the land was theirs, for they
were the Traveling Men, taking their songs and music with them
wherever they'd go.

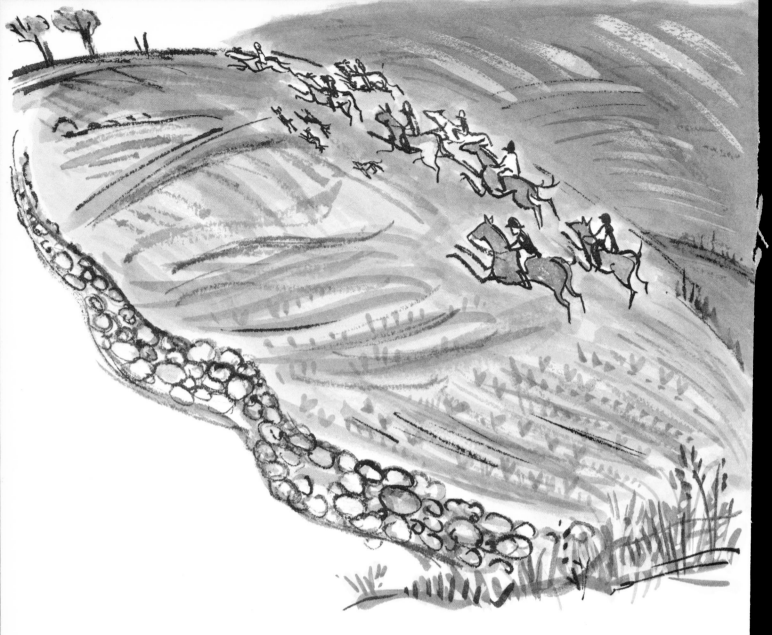

Cathal played the penny whistle. He had a tune called "The Hunt," and in it you could hear, plain as day, the high, wild keen of the hunting horn and the gallop of horses and the bark of dogs as they lit out after the hare. There'd be the sounds of hounds yelping and slavering and, in the end, the terrible squeal of the murdered hare, real enough and true enough to chill the blood in your body. There was many a man heard Cathal play and hung up his boots to hunt no more.

Sean played the fiddle, bent near in two over the top of himself, every bit of him jigging to his music. He'd fiddle so mightily that the resin he rubbed on his bow rose and hung like a mist around his head.

Young Jimmy played the melodeon. He had a tune, a march it was, and you could have sworn a whole brigade of pipers was tramping over the nearest hill, three abreast, their kilts blowing around their bare red knees. All of that came out of a box thing no bigger than a penny loaf.

None of the three was for marriage. Didn't they have all they
needed in each other, with their music to share and a royal
welcome wherever they went?

Cathal always had the right word for everything. "It's the great life we have," he said. "We're taking joy and spreading it from place to place and leaving it behind us when we go. What more could a man ask?"

"Nothing," Sean said.

"Nothing," Young Jimmy agreed.

Maybe it was too great to last forever. It seemed to the
Traveling Men afterwards that the years had gone by without
their noticing them.

Sean was the first to take bad, with the pains in his back. Cathal and Young Jimmy got a fine gray donkey by the name of Mrs. Murphy to carry him. She had eyes, big and shiny as two licked stones, and a back as wide as the valleys between the Mourne Mountains.

When Cathal got the aches in his two legs, Mrs. Murphy was fit enough to hold both him and Sean, and Young Jimmy helped them on and off her back.

The people were still glad to see the Traveling Men. Weren't they the same good boys they'd always been and wasn't their music as fine as ever? They'd be invited in and given mugs of tea. Mrs. Murphy had a corner to herself, and there was always a blanket for Cathal's legs and another for Sean's back and a jar of homemade liniment for them to take along when the music was done for the day and the Traveling Men moved on.

But it was getting harder for them to move on. It was getting harder for them to move.

"There's nothing for it but to settle down," Cathal said. "We'll stop traveling and live in one place, same as everyone else. We're not that young any more."

Which was true. Even Young Jimmy was close to seventy, and he'd lost half of his good, strong teeth.

"It's called making the best of a bad job," Cathal said. Cathal always had the right word for everything.

So they went to Ballycoo.

Simey Rooney's cottage was tight and dry. They settled into it like old birds into a warm nest. In time, they got for themselves a big, soft dog that they called Red Rory and a cow called Maggie and it was surprising how good everything was.

But the evenings were the best. Sean would take out his fiddle and resin up his bow, Cathal would blow a tender breath into his penny whistle, and Jimmy's bent fingers would dance across his melodeon. The notes flew around their heads like quick, white moths, taking away every ache. The fire sparked up the chimney,

and Red Rory slept in its warmth. They'd play "Long Slender
Sally" and "The Dark Woman of the Glen," and sometimes Red
Rory would beat his whiskery tail on the floor and smile in his
sleep while the slow, sweet dusk came settling into night.

They were good times to be sure. But there was something
wanting.

It was Cathal who put the word to it.

"It's right and fine us playing for ourselves and getting the good of it. But we're used to sharing the music we make, and it's not ever as sweet when it's kept to ourselves."

They thought about it, but it was Young Jimmy who had the idea to hang the paper on the door. It said:

MUSIC
NIGHTLY
COME AND
BE
WELCOME

"We'll wait now and see what transpires," Cathal said.

They didn't have long to wait. That very night there came a knock on the door. There were three children outside.

"We heard you playing and we read your notice. Can we come in a wee while and listen?"

"Indeed, and we're glad to have you," Sean told them, and that was that.

Soon the word got out that the greatest Traveling Men that ever were had come to rest in Ballycoo, and there was never a night without music and friends to savor it.

"It's better now, isn't it?" Young Jimmy asked Cathal.

"Aye. Now it's complete," Cathal said.

Sometimes they'd push the settle and stools against the wall and there'd be stepping to "Big John's Reel."

Sometimes there'd be music just for the listening, bringing fairies into the wee warm room . . .

or storms at sea with waves so fierce you were afeared of drowning.

Sometimes you'd be in a forest with the birds singing their shining songs, or you'd be in India, the snake charmer piping his snake like a rope from its curly basket.

One night, when their visitors had gone, the Traveling Men lay side by side in their three feather beds. Rain beat on the outside thatch, and the room was warm with the smell of liniment.

"Since we travel no more, we can't very well be called the Traveling Men, now can we, Cathal?" Jimmy asked sleepily. "What should be the name for us now?"

Cathal scratched at his beard. "Don't we go places every night of our lives, and don't we take all here along with us? Traveling Men we were and are still and always will be."

Young Jimmy smiled and closed his eyes. Cathal always had the right word for everything.